THANKS, DAD. I'M GONNA BE AS GOOD AS GREAT-GRANDMA MING.

I KNOW YOU WILL, DAUGHTER.

YOU'LL BE THE SCOURGE OF THE FOUR KINGS, JUST LIKE YOUR DAD.

BUT NOW, YOUNG RAVEN, IT'S TIME FOR YOU TO JOIN YOUR BROTHERS AND TAKE YOUR BUNK.

DAAAAAAAAAAAD!

NO ARGUMENTS FROM YOU, BOATSWAIN. YOU'VE HAD YOUR STORY, NOW IT'S TIME FOR YOUR REST.

YES, SIR.

NOW, YOU KEEP A LISTEN OUT FOR YOUR BROTHERS. FETCH THE COOK IF THEY NEED ANYTHING.

AYE-AYE, SIR.

TOMORROW WE MAKE A *WARRIOR* OUT OF YOU!

NO HELPLESS *PRINCESS*, MY DAUGHTER.

ISSUE ONE
"GIRLS WHO FIGHT BOYS"
WORDS: Jeremy Whitley
ART: Rosy Higgins & Ted Brandt

SIGH

LIFE JUST NEVER TURNS OUT LIKE YOU *EXPECT.*

Bryan Seaton - Publishe
Kevin Freeman - Preside
Creative Director - Dave Dwonc
Editor In Chief - Shawn Gabbori
Co-Directors of Marketing - Jamal Igle & Kelly Dal
Social Media Director - Jim Die
Education Outreach Director - Jeremy Whitle
Associate Editors - Chad Cicconi & Colleen Boy

NINETY DAYS.

NINETY DAYS I'VE BEEN LOCKED IN THIS TOWER AND NO-ONE HAS EVEN *TRIED* TO RESCUE ME.

POOR PRINCESS RAVEN, NOBODY COMES LOOKING FOR YOU. YOU'RE NOT EVEN A *REAL* PRINCESS.

JUST CALL ME *PRINCESS LAME-O*, JUST STARING OUT YOUR...

HELLO?

HI THERE!

WHAT WAS THAT?

WHO'S THERE?

NOBODY?

FIGURES.

PROBABLY JUST A CLOUD.

HELLO?

AWESOME! LET ME GO PARK MY DRAGON AND I'LL BE RIGHT BACK.

SWEET! YOU SHOULD KNOW THAT THERE'S A KNIGHT DOWN THERE WHO WILL PROBABLY WANT TO FIGHT YOU.

YOU LOOK LIKE YOU NEED TO BE *RESCUED.*

UMM...YES PLEASE, IF YOU DON'T MIND.

NO SWEAT! WE CAN TAKE CARE OF IT. I'M *ADRIENNE ASHE,* BY THE WAY.

I'M *RAVEN XINGTAO.* KICK THEIR BUTT!

RAVEN, YOU SHOULD HURRY.

UH...BEDELIA? I THINK I MADE A MISTAKE.

NONSENSE!

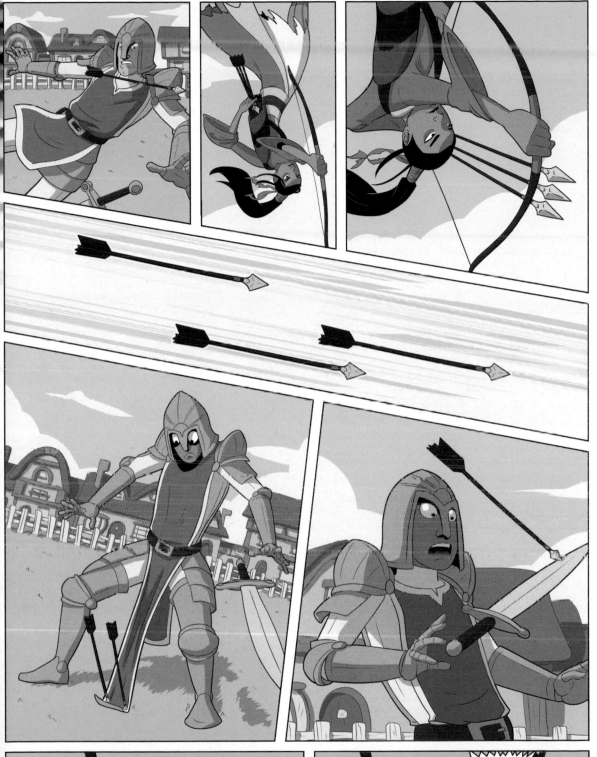

I YIELD!

HA! YOU THOUGHT
THAT WOULD--

WHAT'S GOING ON HERE?

IT'S THE BLACK ARROW!

LET'S GET HER!

HOW DID SHE GET LOOSE?

BEDELIA!

ADRIENNE!

HELP!

UMMM...

LET ME GUESS. THE STEAK SAUCE ISN'T COMING?

I THINK IT'S TIME TO FIGHT AGAIN...AGAIN.

WELL, *BRING IT* THEN.

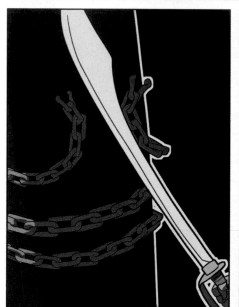

HURRY BEDELIA!

DON'T RUSH ME! THIS THING'S HEAVY!

THAT WAS FUN!

SHOOT, WE DO THAT EVERYWHERE WE GO!

YOU SHOULD JOIN US!

JOIN YOU?

YEAH, WE'RE ON A QUEST TO SAVE MY SISTERS. WE COULD REALLY USE A PIRATE.

AND WE'RE ALREADY WANTED, SO WHAT'S THE HARM?

SOUNDS LIKE FUN...

...NOW, WHERE'S THAT *DRAGON* OF YOURS?

DRAGON-BACK BOXING PRESENTS:

ADRIENNE!
Self-rescuing Princess!

HOLD ON TA
YER HELMETS, IT'S

RAVEN!
The Black Arrow!

★ BRAWLIN' TIME! ★

Introducing
SPARKY
as
THE
ARENA!

DRAGON-BACK BOXING PRESENTS:

 **VS**

ADRIENNE!
Self-rescuing Princess!

**HOLD ON TA
YER HELMETS, IT'S**

RAVEN!
The Black Arrow!

★ BRAWLIN' TIME! ★

Introducing
SPARKY
as
**THE
ARENA!**

SNF

HELLO, DRAGON.

MY NAME IS RAVEN, AND I WANT TO BE YOUR FRIEND.

I'VE NEVER SEEN SPARKY DO THAT. HAVE YOU?

I CAN'T SAY I HAVE.

WHEN I'M AT SEA, I READ A LOT. WE HAD A COUPLE BOOKS ABOUT DRAGONS.

I ALWAYS WANTED TO TRY THAT.

WHAT ABOUT THAT? HAS SHE EVER DONE THAT WITH YOU?

MMM...

SO...WHAT DO WE DO NOW?

LET'S SET UP CAMP. I DON'T WANT TO DO ANY MORE RUNNING OR FIGHTING TONIGHT.

SHOWOFF...

ISSUE TWO
"TWO PRINCESSES GO TO A BRAWL"
WORDS: Jeremy Whitley
ART: Rosy Higgins & Ted Brandt

WOOOHOOOOOOOOOOOOOOOOOOOO!

Bryan Seaton - Publisher
Kevin Freeman - President
Creative Director - Dave Dwonch
Editor In Chief - Shawn Gabborin
Co-Directors of Marketing - Jamal Igle & Kelly Dale
Social Media Director - Jim Dietz
Education Outreach Director - Jeremy Whitley
Associate Editors - Chad Cicconi & Colleen Boyd

THIS IS *AMAZING!* I CAN SEE WHY THEY LOVE IT.

NOW. SPARKY, YOU SEE THAT BIG BLUE AREA OUT THERE? THAT'S THE OCEAN.

MY BROTHERS ARE OUT THERE SOMEWHERE, AND WE'RE GOING TO FIND THEIR SHIPS AND SINK THEM.

THINK AGAIN, TOOTS!

OH, *NO.*

YEAH, "OH NO" IS *RIGHT!*

EN GARDE!

...REALLY? DO PEOPLE ACTUALLY SAY THAT WHERE YOU COME FROM?

I'M NOT GOING TO TOSS YOU OFF, BUT...

PLEASE...

...PRINCESS...

...YOU HAVE *NO IDEA* WHAT YOU'RE GETTING INTO.

I WAS TRAINING TO FIGHT WHILE YOU WERE LEARNING TO CURTSY AND WAVE.

EN GARDE, OR WHATEVER.

THAT'S NOT WHAT A CONTROLLED LUNGE LOOKS LIKE. BAD FORM.

IT LEAVES YOU *VULNERABLE.*

THAT WAS REALLY CUTE, PRINCESS!

DID ONE OF YOUR MAIDS TEACH YOU HOW TO FIGHT?

WAAAAGH!

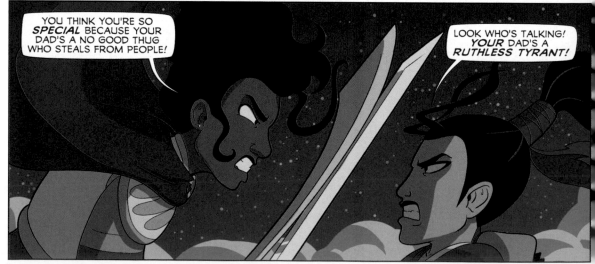

MY DAD ATTACKS THOSE WHO ROB AND CHEAT *THE PEOPLE.*

NO!

HE GIVES TO THE POOR AND HUNGRY.

WHILE THE *GREAT* KING ASHE JUST TAXES THEM TO *DEATH.*

SO DON'T YOU *DARE* TALK BAD ABOUT MY FATHER, YOU STUCK-UP *PRINCESS!*

THAT'S FOR PUNCHING ME, YA *JERK*! I WAS TRYING NOT TO MESS UP YOUR FACE.

WITH A FACE LIKE *YOURS*, I DIDN'T THINK YOU'D MIND!

AND YOU WONDER WHY NO-ONE EVER REALIZES YOU'RE A PRINCESS...

LOOK WHO'S *TALKING!*

WHEN THEY SOLD YOU THAT DRESS THEY MUSTA HID ALL THE MIRRORS!

HARRUUUU!

HAURGH!

YOU'VE GOT THIS, RAVEN. YOU'VE SEEN PEOPLE DO IT BEFORE...

1, 2, 3, 4...

10, 11, 12, 13... COME ON!

COUGH! COUGH!

OH, THANK THE FATES! I THOUGHT... I THOUGHT YOU WERE DONE FOR.

COUGH...COUGH..YOU...

YOU SAVED ME.

LEAST I COULD DO. IT WAS MY FAULT YOU ALMOST DROWNED.

I...I WAS *DEAD* THERE FOR A MOMENT, WASN'T I?

YOU STOPPED BREATHING. LUCKILY, GROWING UP ON A PIRATE SHIP YOU LEARN SOME THINGS.

THAT REALLY COULD HAVE BEEN *IT* FOR ME. RIGHT THERE. NO MORE ADRIENNE.

COME ON, I'M GONNA BUILD US A FIRE SO WE CAN DRY OFF. WE CAN TALK MORE THEN.

I'D LIKE THAT.

WHERE ARE MY CLOTHES?

RAVEN?

BEDELIA?

RAVEN?!

OKAY.

WE RESCUED RAVEN. WE FOUGHT AT THE RESTAURANT. THEN SHE TRIED TO STEAL THE DRAGON. WE FELL IN THE WATER. AND...

I FELL ASLEEP AND LEFT MY ARMOR AND SWORD WITH A *THIEF!*

SHE TRIED TO STEAL MY *DRAGON.*

WHY *WOULDN'T* SHE STEAL MY ARMOR?

SHE'S PROBABLY MILES AWAY BY NOW.

PRINCESS!

COME ON IN! IT'S A GREAT MORNING FOR A SWIM.

UH...

NOW I FEEL STUPID. HOW MUCH OF THAT DID YOU HEAR?

HOW MUCH OF WHAT? I JUST CAME UP - I'VE BEEN SWIMMING.

WERE YOU TALKING TO ME?

NOT EXACTLY...

WHEN YOU WEREN'T THERE AND I COULDN'T FIND MY ARMOR, I ASSUMED YOU'D STOLEN IT AND LEFT ME HERE IN THE WOODS.

I SHOULD HAVE KNOWN BETTER AFTER YOU *SAVED* ME.

HAH!

WELL, TO BE FAIR, I DID TAKE YOUR ARMOR. AND I *DID* LEAVE YOU ALONE WHILE I WENT OUT STEALING.

WHAT?!

TAKE IT EASY, SISTER.

THERE'S A TOWN LESS THAN A MILE ALONG THE BAY FROM HERE.

I STOLE A LITTLE FOOD FOR US, THAT'S ALL.

AS FOR YOUR ARMOR...

IT WAS STILL SOAKED, SO I HUNG IT IN THE TREES TO DRY. IT SHOULD BE GOOD SOON.

YOU DIDN'T NEED TO STEAL FOOD. I HAVE *MONEY.*

OH, I HADN'T REALIZED. WELL, NO HARM.

COME SWIM WITH ME, THEN WE'LL HAVE BREAKFAST.

I DON'T KNOW... AFTER THE SWIM I HAD LAST NIGHT...

KING KALE!!

THAT WATER'S COLD AS AN ELF'S HEART!

HAHAHA!

YOU INLANDERS! I DON'T KNOW HOW YOU NEVER HAVE THE JOY OF A COLD OCEAN SWIM.

PSHH! YOU JUST POINT ME TO THE FOOD. I'LL GET THAT READY WHILE YOU *TURN BLUE...*

CRAZY PIRATE PEOPLE.

YOU WON'T CATCH ANYONE FROM ASHLAND TRYING TO *FREEZE THEMSELVES ALIVE.*

UMMM...

EITHER THIS IS A *LOT* OF FOOD OR...

I'LL TAKE THAT ONE.

I THOUGHT YOU SAID--

AAAAH!

WERE YOU SWIMMING IN THE OCEAN *NAKED?!*

WHAT WOULD *YOU* SUGGEST? WHO BATHES WITH CLOTHES ON?

THAT IS *NOT* A BATH! THAT IS AN OPEN BODY OF WATER! FISH AND SNAKES AND CLAMS *LIVE* IN THERE!

IT'S AMUSING THAT YOU THINK YOUR PALACE WATER IS *CLEANER...*

THE OCEAN IS NATURAL. I WAS BORN THERE. IT'S A PART OF ME.

WHATEVER. IT'S STILL *GROSS.*

ADRIENNE? TURN AROUND AND TELL ME WHAT YOU *THINK...*

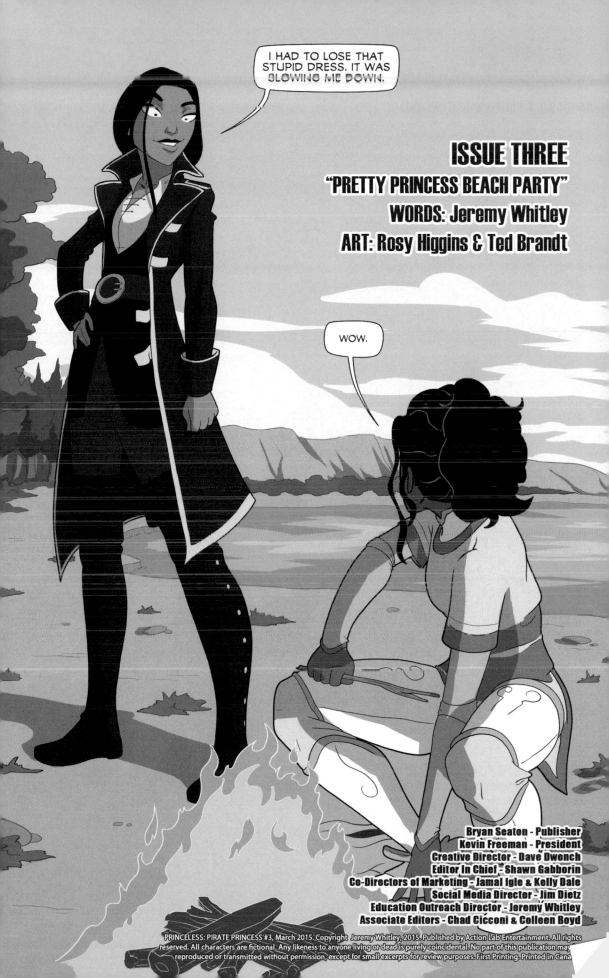

ISSUE THREE
"PRETTY PRINCESS BEACH PARTY"
WORDS: Jeremy Whitley
ART: Rosy Higgins & Ted Brandt

Bryan Seaton - Publisher
Kevin Freeman - President
Creative Director - Dave Dwonch
Editor In Chief - Shawn Gabborin
Co-Directors of Marketing - Jamal Igle & Kelly Dale
Social Media Director - Jim Dietz
Education Outreach Director - Jeremy Whitley
Associate Editors - Chad Cicconi & Colleen Boyd

...I LOOK GOOD?

I THOUGHT YOU ONLY STOLE THE *FOOD!*

OH, I DID. I PAID ALMOST *FULL PRICE* FOR THIS.

YOU LOOK LIKE...

HOW DID YOU *AFFORD* IT? YOU SAID...

ABOUT THE MONEY IN YOUR ARMOR. I MAY HAVE *EXAGGERATED* ABOUT "NOT KNOWING."

YOU STOLE MY MONEY TO BUY *CLOTHES?*

I THINK YOU SHOULD TURN AROUND...

AND YOU DIDN'T BUY *ME* ANY?

NO WAY! YOU DON'T GET OFF THAT EASY!

ADRIENNE...WHAT IS YOUR DRAGON AFRAID OF?

WHAT? WHY?

WHAT WAS *THAT?*

GET YOUR ARMOR ON.

WHY?

BECAUSE THAT'S A *CANNONBALL.*

AND I ONLY KNOW A COUPLE OF MEN *CRAZY* ENOUGH TO FIRE A CANNON AT A DRAGON.

WHERE ARE YOU GOING?

WE'RE GONNA GET ME A *SHIP!*

WHAT?!

JUST LIKE I THOUGHT! IT'S *MAD MOREL*. AND HE LOOKS ANGRY.

...AS THE NAME WOULD SUGGEST.

THE NAME HAS NOTHING TO DO WITH HIS TEMPER.

I SUSPECTED AS MUCH. HE'S WORKING FOR MY BROTHER, *CROW*.

WHY DO THEY CALL HIM...WAIT, IS ALL OF YOUR FAMILY BIRD THEMED?

IT'S A THING. MY MOTHER WAS REALLY INTO POETRY, AND... *ANYWAY.*

I HAVE A *PLAN.* WE CAN OUTFLANK THE SHIP AND STORM THE DECK USING AN OLD FAMILY TRICK.

WAIT! THERE'S A SHIP *FULL* OF ANGRY, *ARMED* PIRATES OUT THERE...

...AND YOU'RE SUGGESTING WE *GET ON IT?!*

DO YOU UNDERSTAND, SPARKY? CANNONS ARE SLOW. AS LONG AS YOU DON'T FLY STRAIGHT AT THE SHIP THEY CAN'T *HIT* YOU.

YEAH, LET'S TEACH THEM A LESSON ABOUT PICKING ON INNOCENT DRAGONS.

HUFF.

WE GO IN *FIVE.*

WAIT, *WHY* DO THEY CALL HIM MAD MOREL?

BECAUSE HE'S A TOTAL *PSYCHO.*

I WANT THREE OVER HERE AND FOUR IN THE BACK.

DO IT *NOW!*

SIR, COULDN'T HAVING ALL OF THESE CANNONS ON OUR DECK--

ARE YOU *QUESTIONING* ME, YOU BELLIGERENT BUFFOON?!

NO, SIR, CAP'N MOREL.

GOOD, NOW GET THOSE CANNONS *READY!* WE'RE GONNA TAKE THAT DRAGON OUT OF THE SKY!

LET'S SEE IF THE MONKEYS STILL THINK THEY CAN KEEP EYES ON ME AFTER I TAKE DOWN THEIR *SPY!*

THEY'LL NEVER GET *ME*... NO, THEY WON'T...

I GUESS THIS IS A GOOD A TIME AS ANY TO MENTION THAT SPARKY'S FLYING IS NOT VERY *ACCURATE.*

SHE TENDS TO MISS HER TARGET A LOT.

THAT'S NOT TRUE, IS IT, SPARKY?

GUFF LUFF.

ALRIGHT, SPARKY, COME HERE.

HERE'S THE DEAL, SPARKY:

MY BROTHERS TOOK EVERYTHING I *HAD* FROM ME AND LEFT ME *LOCKED IN A TOWER.*

AS WE *SPEAK,* THERE IS NO TELLING WHAT OTHER *NONSENSE* THEY ARE PUTTING IN MY DAD'S HEAD. HIS LIFE COULD DEPEND ON ME.

GETTING THIS SHIP FROM THESE BAD MEN IS THE FIRST STEP IN SAVING EVERYTHING IN MY LIFE THAT MEANS *ANYTHING.*

IF WE'RE GOING TO DO THIS, YOU'RE GOING TO HAVE TO FLY LIKE YOU'VE NEVER FLOWN BEFORE.

CAN I *COUNT* ON YOU?

RUFF!

THATTA GIRL.

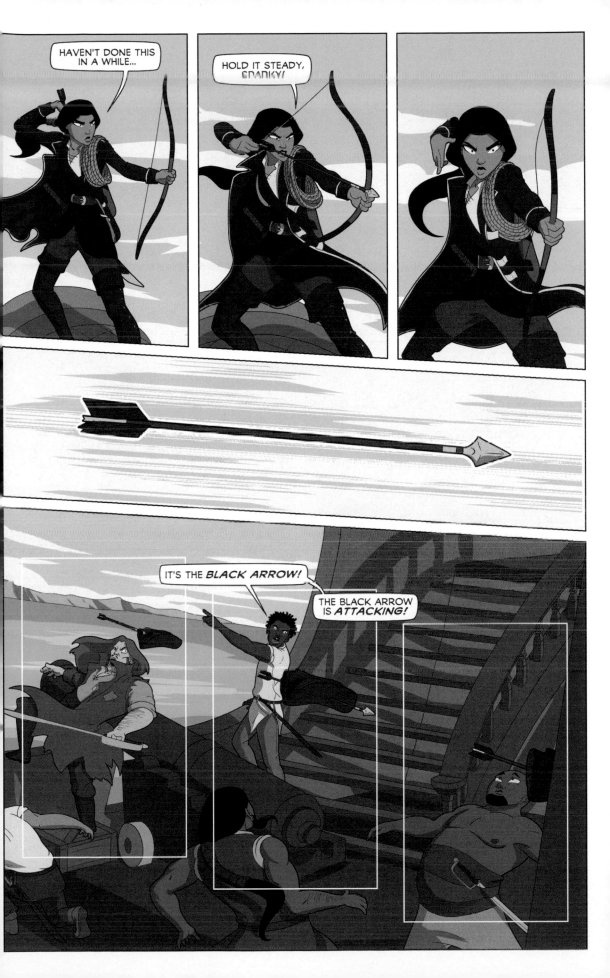

YES!

I STILL GOT IT!

I WAS ON A DRAGON AND THEY WERE ON A BOAT AND THEY WERE SHOOTING AT US AND THE WIND IS BLOWING AND WE'RE BOTH MOVING AND *BAM!*

HAT RIGHT OFF HIS HEAD!

RAVEN! *RAVEN!*

THERE'S STILL THE LITTLE MATTER OF GETTING ON AND TAKING OVER THE PIRATE SHIP!

OH, THAT? THAT SHOULD BE *EASY.*

CLEVER RUSE, MONKEYS, BUT I KNOW THE BLACK ARROW AND SHE'S NO MONKEY LACKEY!

WHO'S THIS IMPOSTER?

SPARKY! MY HERO!

I'M GONNA THROW UP. SPIRALS ARE *BAD*.

HOLD IT IN JUST A BIT LONGER. TIE THIS ROPE TO THE SADDLE.

I WANT TO GO BACK TO THE BEACH...

WE'LL HAVE YOU BACK THERE SOON.

YOU READY?

LET'S DO THIS.

THE *BLACK ARROW* IS BACK!

WAAGH!

SIGH.

RAVEN... A LITTLE HELP, PLEASE?

YOU WERE SUPPOSED TO LET GO *BEFORE* YOU GOT TO THE MAST.

WELL YOU DIDN'T TELL ME THAT!

I FIGURED YOU'D KNOW THAT YOU *DIDN'T* WANT TO RUN FACE FIRST INTO A SHIP!

I DIDN'T HAVE A LOT OF TIME TO THINK ABOUT THAT WHILE YOU WERE TRYING TO THROW A *DRAGON* AT A *BOAT!*

I KNOW YOU'RE USED TO HAVING SERVANTS THAT CUT YOUR FOOD AND *CHEW* FOR YOU...

...BUT I THOUGHT YOU'D HAVE SOME COMMON SENSE.

YEAH, WELL... SHUT UP! THIS IS YOUR FAULT!

ARE YOU READY NOW?

HOLD ON, I HAD A LINE!

GO ON, THEN...

LAME.

"AND SHE BROUGHT *FRIENDS!*"

MY NAME IS **RAVEN XINGTAO**, AND I AM A **PIRATE**. THAT DOESN'T MEAN THE SAME THING TO EVERY-BODY, SO LET ME EXPLAIN.

OUR LAND IS RULED BY MERCILESS **WARLORD KINGS**; THEY TAX THEIR PEOPLE INTO POVERTY SO THEY CAN AFFORD TO SEND THEM OFF TO **DIE IN WARS**.

GENERATIONS AGO, MY FAMILY DECIDED TO **DEFEND** THE PEOPLE AGAINST THESE RUTHLESS LORDS.

SO THE **BARON AND BARONESS XINGTAO** OF THE **NORTH PENINSULA** RAISED AN ARMY OF VOLUNTEERS AND BATTLED TO FREE THE LAND OF THE NORTH PENINSULA FROM THE **HIGH KING**.

THEIR BRAVERY AND MIGHT BROUGHT THE PEOPLE TOGETHER TO PUSH BACK AGAINST THE CROWN.

ALAS, THEIR ARMY WAS A FRACTION OF THE SIZE OF THE KING'S, AND NOT NEARLY AS WELL EQUIPPED.

IT WAS ONLY DUE TO THE HELP OF THE SERVANTS THEY HAD FREED THAT THE BARON AND BARONESS WERE ABLE TO **ESCAPE** INTO THE WOODS.

BUT EVEN THAT RESPITE DID NOT LAST LONG. THE **KING'S MEN** FOUND THEM.

THE BARON WAS TERRIBLY WOUNDED...

BUT THE KNIGHTS UNDERESTIMATED THE BARONESS' SKILL WITH A SWORD. THAT WAS A MISTAKE THEY WOULD **NOT** LIVE TO REPEAT.

THE BARONESS SWORE THAT AS LONG AS THEIR LINE CONTINUED, THEY WOULD FIGHT AGAINST TYRANNY.

THE BARONESS KNEW THAT THEY DID NOT HAVE THE MANPOWER TO FIGHT ON LAND; BUT ON THE *SEA*, AS PIRATES, THE XINGTAO FAMILY COULD HAUNT THE KING.

AND THAT'S WHERE *I* COME IN.

MY FATHER HAS BEEN LEADING A FLEET OF PIRATES FOR YEARS. UNDER HIS WATCH, THE FLEET GREW MASSIVE IN SIZE. THEY CALLED HIM THE *PIRATE KING.*

AS THE *OLDEST*, THE FLEET AND THAT WAR WERE TO BE MY *INHERITANCE.*

BUT MY YOUNGER BROTHERS, *CROW* AND *MAGPIE*, WERE NOT HAPPY TO BE SECOND AND THIRD. THEY PLANTED THE SEEDS OF DISCONTENT IN MY FATHER'S MIND.

IF HE WAS "THE PIRATE KING," HE SHOULD HAVE A *PROPER* HEIR AND A LEGACY TO LEAVE BEHIND.

...AND IF HE WAS A KING, THAT MADE ME A *PRINCESS.*

WHICH IS HOW I CAME TO BE LOCKED IN A TOWER, AWAITING *RESCUE* FROM A HANDSOME PRINCE.

AND HOW I ENDED UP BEING RESCUED BY THE DAUGHTER OF MY FAMILY'S SWORN ENEMY, *KING ASHE.*

AND HOW I ENDED UP *ASSAULTING* ONE OF MY OWN BROTHER'S SHIPS.

CAPTAIN MOREL.

THIS SHIP AND CREW ARE *MINE* BY RIGHT AND SWORN TO MY FAMILY'S SERVICE. I ORDER YOU TO TURN OVER CONTROL *AT ONCE*.

HMPH.

THIS SHIP IS UNDER MY COMMAND BY THE AUTHORITY OF YOUR BROTHER, *THE CROW*. IF YOU HAVE ISSUE, I SUGGEST YOU TAKE IT UP WITH HIM.

I *AIM* TO.

YOU'VE SERVED MY FATHER FOR YEARS. YOU KNOW THAT I'M THE *RIGHTFUL* HEIR.

SO, THE BLACK ARROW AIMS TO TAKE WHAT HER BROTHERS *OWN*?

YOU'D BETTER HAVE COME READY TO *FIGHT*.

MEN! GET THIS WHINY GIRL OFFA *MY SHIP*!

Bryan Seaton - Publisher
Kevin Freeman - President
Creative Director - Dave Dwonch
Editor In Chief - Shawn Gabborin
Co-Directors of Marketing - Jamal Igle & Kelly Dale
Social Media Director - Jim Dietz
Education Outreach Director - Jeremy Whitley
Associate Editors - Chad Cicconi & Colleen Boyd

HUH?

WHAT HAPPENED?

THE CANNONS! WHEN THEY FIRE THEY SHOOT ACROSS THE DECK!

WELL, THAT'S GREAT FOR HER, BUT IT LEAVES TWICE AS MANY FOR ME!

COME ON THEN! LET'S *DO* THIS!

RUN!

THAT'S RIGHT!

RUN FROM ADRIENNE, *BATTLE PRINCESS!*

YOU DON'T STAND A *CHANCE* AGAINST MY--

POOP.

WHAT?!

IT'S WOOD, GIRL...

I'VE BEEN FIGHTING ONE-LEGGED SINCE YOU WERE IN DIAPERS.

NOW TO SEND A MESSAGE TO THOSE *MONKEYS* THAT SENT YOU!

MONKEYS?

THEY'RE IN THE *TREES* EVERY TIME I'M ON LAND. *WATCHING.*

THAT'S JUST WHAT *THEY* SAY! THOSE MONKEYS WANT ME TO THINK THAT!

MOREL, YOU REALLY ARE MAD!

NOW, LITTLE GIRL...

DO YOU SEE THE MISTAKE YOU MADE?

YOU'RE UNARMED. YOU'RE *WEAK.*

YOU HAVE NO BUSINESS AT THE HEAD OF THIS FLEET.

YOU'RE THE ONE MAKING THE MISTAKE.

ALL OF YOU SAW WHAT *HAPPENED* HERE? SAY "AYE, BLACK ARROW!"

AYE, BLACK ARROW!

AM I THE GREATEST AND STRONGEST PIRATE?

AM I THE *RIGHTFUL* HEIR TO THE PIRATE KING'S FLEET?

AYE, BLACK ARROW!

GOOD!

MAKE SURE YOU TELL MY *BROTHERS* WHEN YOU GET BACK TO LAND.

NOW...

GET OFF MY SHIP!

I'M SORRY ABOUT YOUR BROTHERS. IT SOUNDS LIKE THEY'RE AS BAD AS MY *SISTERS.*

YOUR SISTERS STOLE YOUR LIFE'S AMBITION AND TOLD A GROUP OF RUTHLESS PIRATES TO KILL YOU ON SIGHT?

NOT EXACTLY. THEY'RE ALL JUST... WELL, THEY MAKE ME FEEL AWFUL.

THEY'RE ALL SO PRETTY AND SO... I DON'T KNOW.

THEY JUST MAKE ME FEEL LIKE I'M WEIRD.

ADRIENNE, LISTEN TO ME.

YOU ARE *AMAZING.* EVERYTHING ABOUT YOU IS AMAZING AND IF THAT MEANS YOU'RE WEIRD, THEN WEIRD IS THE BEST THING I CAN IMAGINE A GIRL *BEING.*

RAVEN...

AND BEYOND THAT, I THINK YOU'RE GORGEOUS.

I CAN'T BELIEVE WE SPENT SO MUCH TIME FIGHTING! I WISH YOU WERE MY SISTER.

SISTER?

MY SISTERS NEVER DO ANYTHING BUT NITPICK EVERYTHING ABOUT ME.

IT'S NICE TO HEAR ANOTHER GIRL SAY NICE THINGS ABOUT ME AND NOT JUST SOME GUY WHO'S SAYING IT BECAUSE HE LIKES ME.

YEAH, RIGHT, I GET THAT.

WHAT DO YOU SAY, WANT AN HONORARY SISTER?

I GUESS I CAN LIVE WITH THAT. I'VE NEVER HAD A SISTER BEFORE.

SO WHAT NOW? WHAT'S NEXT FOR THE *PIRATE PRINCESS?*

EURGH! DON'T CALL ME THAT. THAT'S A STUPID TITLE.

I'M WORRIED ABOUT WHAT MAD MOREL SAID. IF SOMETHING HAPPENED TO MY DAD...

BUT ISN'T HE THE ONE WHO PUT YOU IN THAT TOWER TO BEGIN WITH?

YEAH, SORTA, BUT HE WAS GOING THROUGH SOME THINGS.

I DON'T BLAME HIM. I GUESS IT'S LIKE YOU WANTING TO SAVE YOUR SISTERS, RIGHT? YOU SAID YOU GUYS HAVE SOME ISSUES.

I GUESS.

BEDELIA WILL BE SAD SHE DIDN'T GET TO SEE YOU OFF. SHE AND SPARKY REALLY LIKED YOU.

THEY REALLY LIKE YOU TOO. THAT'S WHY THEY'RE FOLLOWING YOU.

YEAH, I GUESS.

HUH?

ADRIENNE, I KNOW YOU'RE ON A QUEST, BUT DO SOMETHING FOR ME.

DON'T WEAR THE ARMOR ALL THE TIME. THE GIRL UNDER IT IS PRETTY GREAT.

THANKS. I SHOULD GET BACK. BEDELIA'S PROBABLY PANICKING.

BYE, LITTLE SISTER.

BYE, BIG SISTER.

ZZZZZZSNORT

Take a deep breath. Feel the wind in your hair and the sun on your face.

Breathe out the thought of **everything** else but your mission.

And when you're ready, raise your **bow**.

Easy now. You've got time, girl.

Make the first shot count.

Good.

Take aim. Measure the wind.

And when you're ready...

Release.

ISSUE ONE
"CHASING SUNSHINE"
WORDS: Jeremy Whitley
PENCILS/COLORS: Rosy Higgins
LAYOUTS/INKS/
LETTERS: Ted Brandt

My name is Raven Xingtao, but you may know me as the Black Arrow.

My father is the Pirate King, and I was meant to inherit that position.

But my brothers took what was mine, and had me locked in a tower to await a prince.

Two weeks ago, I was rescued from my tower; tried to steal a dragon; succeeded in stealing a ship.

I used to be the future Queen, until I lost everything.

Bryan Seaton - Publisher
Kevin Freeman - President
Creative Director - Dave Dwonch
Editor In Chief - Shawn Gabborin
Co-Directors of Marketing - Jamal Igle & Kelly Dale
Social Media Director - Jim Dietz
Education Outreach Director - Jeremy Whitley
Associate Editors - Chad Cicconi & Colleen Boyd

And now I'm going to get it back...

Huh. Old ghosts. I'm seventeen and already I have old ghosts.

Where are you, daddy?

Where are any of those good men?

Where's...

At least you're not that far gone, shippy.

I can bring you back from what Morel did to you.

KNOCK KNOCK

Rotten...

bug-infested...

piece of--

CHUCK CHUCK

Hyuh!

Okay. I didn't think this through. Revenge is one thing.

I'm ready to bring my brothers down, but...

...they're at sea on their own little islands--

(Father's islands, which should be mine)

--and I can't get to them to take my revenge without a crew.

And how do I even get one of those?

Father always just had men around, but now they're with my brothers.

Why did I ever let that princess and dwarf girl go? Well, I know--

Gah!

Aagh!

KATIE COOK
VARIANT